This Walker book

belongs to:

. . . . . . . . . . . . . . . . . . . . . . . .

. . . . . . . . . . . . . . . . . . . . .

. . . . . . . . . . . . . . . . . . . . . .

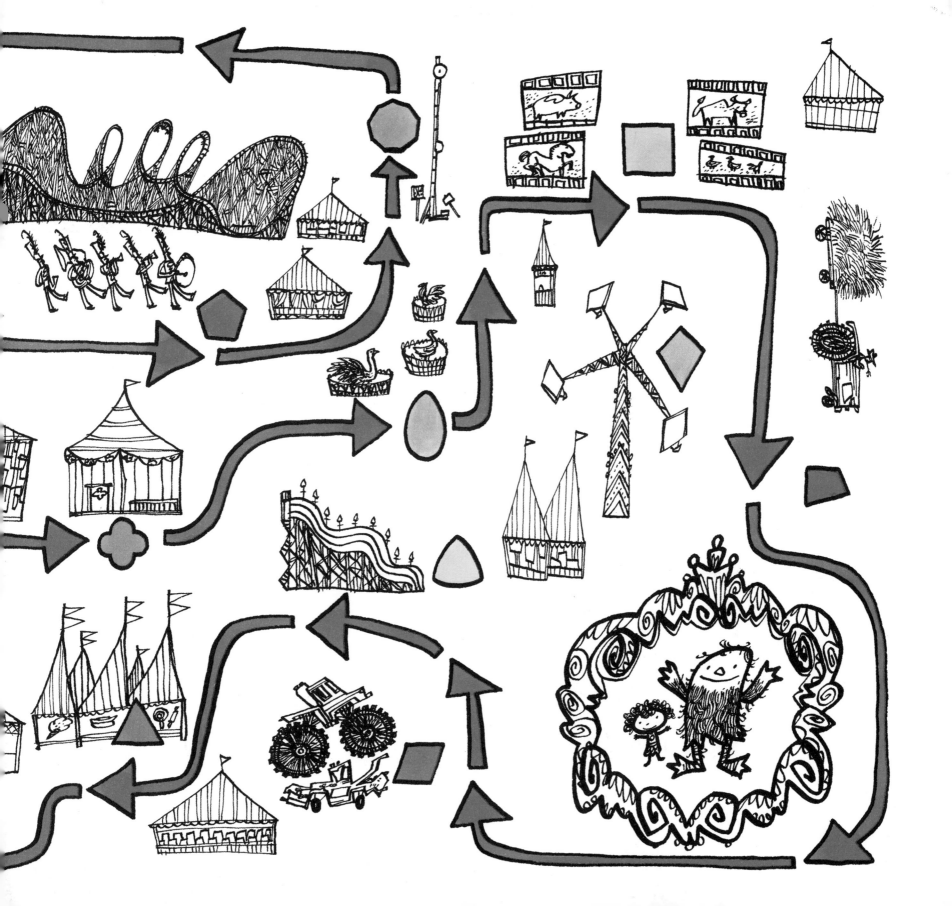

To the country kids:
Taylor, Karl Patrick, Ava and Gabriel

First published 2015 by Walker Books Ltd
87 Vauxhall Walk, London SE11 5HJ

2 4 6 8 10 9 7 5 3 1

This edition published 2016

© 2015 Steve Light

The right of Steve Light to be identified as author/illustrator of this work has been
asserted by him in accordance with the Copyright, Designs and Patents Act 1988

This book has been typeset in Stempel Schneidler

Printed in China

British Library Cataloguing in Publication Data: a catalogue record
for this book is available from the British Library

ISBN 978-1-4063-6594-8

www.walker.co.uk

# Have You Seen My MONSTER?

## STEVE LIGHT

WALKER BOOKS
AND SUBSIDIARIES
LONDON · BOSTON · SYDNEY · AUCKLAND

# Have you seen my monster?

No? Maybe he's already at the fair.

He loves the carousel…

Did he go to judge the pies?

He loves the fun house …

hexagon

and the bearded lady.

If he went to the egg display, I hope he's careful!

Maybe he went to see
the livestock. I hope he doesn'
scare the animals.

square

kite ◆

Can you see my monster?

Has my monster been on this ride?

trapezium

# MONSTER TRUCK CRASH!

Wheeeeeeee!

triangle △

My monster may have needed a snack.

Maybe he –
*bump,*
        *bump,*
*bump*
came here.

heptagon

Perhaps I can see him from up here!

trapezoid

He's very good at crafts …

maybe he won a prize!

He loves music!

pentagon

**nonagon**

Where could he be?

Maybe up high …

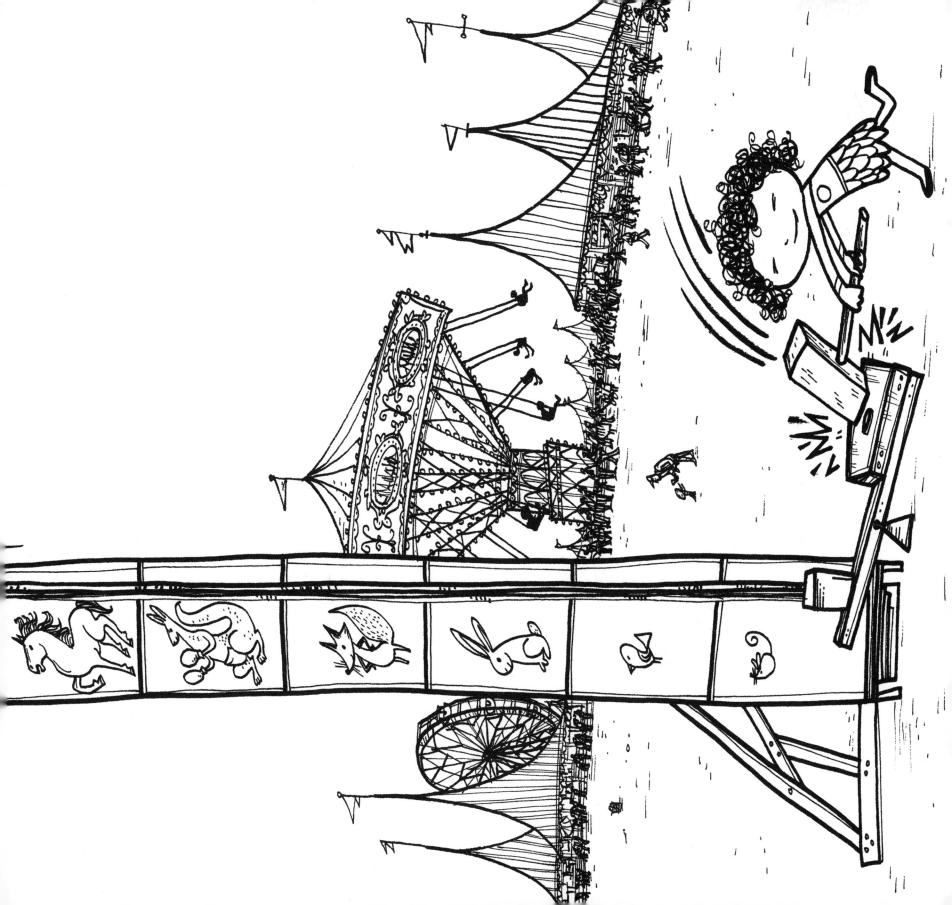

or just hanging out!

Oh, there he is!

decagon

Time to take my monster home.

crescent